How to Have a Positive Attitude for Kids

By:

Caleb Maddix

Book Cover Design: Caleb Maddix

Editing: Amy Kochek

Printing and/or ordering information:

amazon.com

Table of Contents

1

Your Choice

WWWHHHHHHHHAAAAAAAATTTTTTT T's up Maddix Addicts! I've been hearing from many of you that are reading my books, and I'm so proud of what you all have accomplished thus far. Some of you have set and achieved massive goals, and I am really impressed. Change is not easy, but like I always say, when information is turned into application, transformation is guaranteed.

Get ready, guys! This book is going to make a great impact in your lives. Each of my books is designed to dive deep and get more intense with the valuable content.

I believe that the concept of positivity is so powerful because it literally changed my life forever. In fact, I realized that as I began to master positivity, every area of my life started to improve. That is the power of positivity.

You see, the world is full of negativity. If you don't believe me, turn on the news. I can almost guarantee that most of what you will see and hear will be negative. News reporters will tell you about tragedies, crimes, wars, disagreements, and sadness that is going on in the world right now.

In addition to that, most of our friends, family, teachers, coaches, and just flat out most of the people we know are negative people. Negativity can come from what we watch, eat, listen to, or talk about. There is usually a source of negativity that each person must overcome.

I must confess that when I was younger, I was a negative kid. As I said before, there is a source of negativity, and for me, it came from a close friendship I had at school.

When I was in school, I remember there was this one kid in my class who was extremely and unbelievably negative. During PE, he complained about all his assigned sports teams. After receiving his test scores, he would complain that the teacher didn't teach well. He even complained about the gifts he was given. I only saw him for a few hours each day at school, so I can't even imagine what he was like at home.

One day, after hearing another one of his familiar complaint sessions, I decided to do some investigating. It was kind of bugging me how negative he was because at the time, I considered myself to be somewhat positive. I decided to just ask him a direct question, so I went up to him and said, "Dude, why are you so negative?"

At first, he seemed shocked. Perhaps no one had ever asked him this question. After about a minute, he gave me an answer that really left an impression on my life. He said, "Caleb, I'm so negative because I don't have a choice. I mean look at my life. It is just so unfair." Then, for the next 20 minutes, he started telling me about his family problems, struggles with his grades, bullies at school, arguments he had with his parents, and the stuff he didn't have that he wished he did.

After he finished, I didn't really know what to say because I had similar complaints. I realized that he was kind of right. Life was unfair for me as well, and nothing seemed to go my way either. My home life wasn't always the best; my parents didn't give me exactly what I wanted; school was frustrating at times; my baseball coach always made me mad; and I felt like I needed more.

My conversation with this kid affected me so much, that I couldn't get it off my mind. For two weeks, my thoughts and actions began to change. The phrase, "Life is just so unfair," stayed in my mind. In addition, my mood, behavior, grades, and interactions with other people drastically changed as well. I became an unpleasant person to be around.

My dad noticed this major shift in my attitude. Because he wanted me to understand the power of a positive mindset, he had me watch Tony Robbins' motivational speech on positivity. In this video, Tony gave a powerful analogy. He told everyone in the audience to close their eyes. Then he said, "When I say go, I want you to open your eyes, look around the room, and find every single thing that is purple. Then, when I tell you to close your eyes, we'll close them together." Even though I wasn't in the physical audience during the live speech, I decided to participate.

When Tony said, "Go!" I opened my eyes and looked around the room. I saw purple paintings, purple dishes, purple pillows, and some shades of purple on the pair of tennis shoes I was wearing.

After a few moments, Tony told us to close our eyes again, so I closed them. Then he said, "Okay, now I want you to tell me everything in the room that was red." Everyone in the audience laughed, and as I sat on my couch, I joined in that laughter. Despite the laughter, Tony said, "No really, tell me everything in the room that was red."

The first thought that went through my mind was, "What is Tony talking about? He told us to focus on everything that was purple, so I was only looking for anything that was purple. How would I know what was red?" My thought was interrupted when Tony said, "Okay, now when I tell you to open your eyes again, I want you to look for everything that is red." When he said go, I opened my eyes and started looking around the room for everything that was red. I saw the red TV stand, my dad's red shoes, and the red cars outside of our apartment.

When Tony told us that time was up, he asked us a second time to identify all the red objects we saw. My reaction was different this time because I had a list of red objects that I saw. Tony, then asked us a question. "Why did you see more stuff that was red the second time?" I thought, "Well, it's because I was focusing on finding red objects."

Tony used this analogy to teach a secret of positivity. If you spend every day looking for all the things that are going wrong, that is all you will see. However, if you spend every day looking for all the things that are going right, that is all you will see.

I applied the information and used this point to start focusing on what was going right in my life. As my focus changed, I immediately started seeing the positive parts of my life. I thought, "I have great parents; I'm good at sports; I enjoy my school environment; I don't get bullied all that much; and I'm healthy and in good shape. Also, I get to live in Florida where the weather is great!" Once I started thinking of all these things that were going right in my life, I realized that I was living a great life.

In the video, Tony said something memorable. He said, "No matter what you focus on, that's what you will see." He also pointed out that every single person has a choice to become positive or negative. That choice is called perspective.

Perspective means the way you view something or a situation. For instance, let's say you get a bad grade on a test. One perspective would see the negative. You can complain about the teacher, get sad that this grade will affect your overall grade, and be upset that your parents may not be pleased. Another perspective would see the positive. This bad grade can be used to motivate you to work harder. It can help you build persistence and improve your study skills. Changing your perspective doesn't change the situation, it just makes it easier to have a positive attitude in spite of the situation.

Hearing Tony tell the audience that they could choose negativity or positivity made me realize that I was able to choose too. Not only that, I realized that my super negative friend had a choice as well. He was wrong when he told me he had no choice but to be negative. I had a choice, he had a choice, and you have a choice. We can choose to focus on the positive, or we can focus on the negative.

Here is the great news. You don't need a magic potion to help you become positive. Keep that stuff in fairy tales. Your magic potion is simply called perspective. You can become a positive kid when you realize that you are in control of your negativity and positivity.

After I watched this video, I was excited about applying more of the information. I started using a positive perspective in school. Anytime something bad would happen, I would think of something positive to gain from the situation. For example, anytime I would get on a bad team in PE, I would think about how I could help the other members of the team so we could become better. Anytime I received a poor grade, I would figure out ways to study more effectively and challenge myself to get a better grade on the next assignment. I tried to take something as simple as a rainy day and make it positive. If it started to rain, I would come up with activities that I could only do in the rain and do them.

Remember, you have a choice to become a negative or positive kid, and before we move on with this book, you must choose. It is not going to be easy because like I said before, sometimes it can seem like we are surrounded by negativity. On the other hand, if you use the strategies and tools that I'm going to provide in this book, the choice for daily positivity will become easy. You must choose what you are going to focus on every day.

Let's decide right now to shift our perspective towards the positive. Yeah, things could be better in everybody's life. There will always be room for improvement, but we are going to choose to focus on this moment. You and I are alive, breathing, reading, learning, and growing. That alone is motivation to live a positive life. So, are you ready? Of course, you are! You are a champion, and you are ready to master this skill of positivity. Let's start the journey.

2

Go the Extra Smile

I want to start with an activity that we can do together. Grab two sheets of paper. On one piece of paper, I want you to write the words, "super negative person," at the top. On the other piece of paper, I want you to write the words, "super positive person" at the top. Now, gather some art supplies like markers and colored pencils because we are going to draw pictures of what a negative and positive person look like. Before we start drawing, think about this question. What do you think a negative person looks like? For instance, when I think of a negative person, I imagine that he is probably frowning, slouching, tired, and talks quietly. Using these descriptions, I would draw a person that has these characteristics. Just like I did, start to visualize what a negative person looks like and draw that image on the paper.

Once you complete the negative paper, get the other piece of paper and do that same thing for the positive picture. Before you draw, think about this question. "What does a positive person look like?" Well, when I think about a positive person, he probably has a smile on his face, talks enthusiastically, stands up straight, and his eyes would probably be a little bit wrinkly because he smiles so much. Now, it's your turn to draw your image on the positive side.

After your pictures are complete, put them side by side. I am almost certain that there will be some specific differences between the two images. Pay close attention to the picture you drew of the negative person. When you thought of the negative person, maybe you thought of someone that was frowning with poor posture.

On the other hand, the picture of the positive image may have a smile on his face, standing up straight and looking confident. Do you see how powerful the differences are? Look closely at the positive person's face and focus on his smile for a minute.

I'm going to share a key to positivity that may seem weird. Smiling people are positive people. Even though positive people smile, they do not have to feel positive to smile. I've said this phrase before, but I think it is worth repeating. "You don't feel your way into acting, you act your way into feeling."

To further show you a smile's powerful connection to positivity, we are going to do another activity together. I want you to smile as big as you can. I mean really show your teeth. Hopefully, you've brushed your teeth today. Lol! Next, find your favorite upbeat song and make sure the volume is up high. (Note: Don't blast your music if your parents are asleep or if it is an inappropriate time of the day). Wait! Before you hit play, I have further instructions. When I say, "go," start the song, keep that huge smile on your face, and start jumping up and down in time with the beat. Ready? Go!

How do you feel? Since I've done this activity before, I will assume that you are slightly out of breath, your heart rate is up and you still have a smile on your face.

We are going to change it up a bit now. Stop smiling and start to frown. Look at yourself in the mirror while you are doing this. Notice the change in your entire face when you went from a smile to a frown. With a frown still on your face, find a place to sit down and slouch in the chair. How do you feel? I can assume that your heart rate is slower, your energy has decreased, and your mood may have changed.

Now, I'm going to ask you a final question in this activity. Which actions felt better? Smiling and jumping up and down, or frowning and slouching in your seat? I know my answer to this question because when I did this activity in my room, I felt better smiling and jumping up and down. Notice that I did not give you a reason to smile or jump up and down. You did it because I told you, and you had a positive reaction. It may sound simple, but a key to living a positive life is your smile." And remember, your smile does not have to be connected to a positive feeling. Let me explain this a little further.

Years ago, I was introduced to a principle of positivity called, "acting as if." This means that even when you do not *feel* positive, you can *act* as if you're positive. You may be feeling negative and down, but if you smile in spite of it, you will notice your mood begin to change. Your smile may cause you to think of a good memory or funny joke. In moments, your mood can change because of your smile. That is powerful. When I learned this principle, I put it into immediate action and received some amazing results.

Throughout the next day in school, any time I was feeling down or upset, I would just smile. I wouldn't force it, but I would smile with my whole face to include my eyes. To encourage my smile, there would be times that I would kind of think of something funny. I even had moments that I started to laugh. When the day was complete, I realized that not only did I have one of the most positive days I've ever had, but other people responded to me in a more positive way as well. To think that this level of positivity began with just a smile.

I can't emphasize the importance of smiling enough. I want you guys to do something real quick. Yeah, that's right, you. While you're reading this, I want you to smile super big. Don't just put your mouth in the shape of a smile, but I want you to exaggerate it. Smile as big as possible. Okay, are you doing it? Okay, great. Now I want you to keep the smile and exaggeration, but I want you to feel mad. Okay, are you smiling really big? Are you also trying to feel mad? Do you notice something? It's impossible to smile and feel mad at the same time. That's because smiling is the number one enemy of negativity. You defeat negativity with a smile, and you defeat positivity when you lose your smile.

I want you to start using the, "acting as if" tool. Any time you don't feel good, smile really big. If you need help smiling, think of something that's funny. You're not convinced on the importance of smiling yet? Well, let me tell about a guy named Norman Cousins.

Norman Cousins was an older man that had a disease that was slowly killing him. The doctors told him he had a short time to live. He was so sick that he had to stay in the hospital. All his friends and family focused on the sadness surrounding his soon coming death. Norman Cousins started to focus on his death as well. He became depressed and most of his days in the hospital were filled with negativity. But then one day he thought, "Well, if I'm going to die, then I might as well die laughing. I can't waste my last days filled with sadness."

To increase his positivity, he watched super funny videos every single night. Then, he started watching funny videos for seven to eight hours a day. He spent most of his days and nights laughing. The other patients were becoming upset with him because his laughter kept them up at night. Even the doctors tried to discourage his laughter. Despite the opinion of others, Norman continued to laugh. Two weeks later, a miracle occurred. The doctors did a scan to check the progress of his illness, but it was completely gone. Norman defeated the illness that was supposed to kill him, and his main form of attack was laughter. Later, he was asked what the key to overcoming his illness was, and his only response was, "I laughed."

I truly believe this. I think the number one cause of most illnesses is a lack of laughter and smiling. Grab your drawing of the super positive person and turn it over. On the backside of this paper, I want you to make two columns. On the left side of the paper, write out a list of things that make you laugh or automatically smile. On the right side of the paper, write out a list of things that you can do that will make you smile or lift your mood.

Now, anytime you're feeling negative, I want you to look at that list and start thinking or doing some of the things you wrote. If playing music or dancing crazy makes you laugh, then do it when you're feeling negative. Maybe there was a funny experience you had with your parents, siblings, or friends. When you're not feeling good, try to focus on that experience instead of your current mood. I promise you, your negativity is going to shrink, and it all starts with smiling.

I like to think of it this way. Laughter for the mind is like jogging for the body. The people who jog the most are going to be the healthiest. Similarly, the people who smile the most are going to be the most positive. Not only that, but have you ever heard of the saying, "go the extra mile"? Let me ask you a question. Who is going to be healthier, someone who jogs two miles a day or someone who jogs three miles a day? It's going to be the person that goes the extra mile. They're going to get the extra results. They're going to be extraordinary. In the same way, if you want to be the most positive, then you need to go the extra smile. I promise you, the person who laughs the most throughout the day will be the one who's the most positive. The person that is the most positive will receive greater results.

Since you understand the power of a smile, let's spread this message to our community and the millions on social media that need some positivity.

Take a minute to go get your phone out. Put on your best smile, and like I said earlier, don't just put your mouth in the shape of a smile. Think of something funny or watch a funny video if you need some more motivation. When you get that real big smile, take a picture or video. Show me your best smile and laugh. Afterwards, post it on social media and use the hashtags #PositivityWins #MaddixAddict.

Let's start a positivity movement. There is so much negativity being posted online. The only way to change that is to drown out the noise of negativity with our positive words and smiles. So, what are you waiting for? Go the extra smile and take the most important step towards become a positive kid.

3

Work Your Positivity Muscle

Imagine that you were told that you had to sit in a wheelchair for 1 year. You wouldn't be able to walk or use your legs for anything the entire year. Once the year was complete, you tried to get out of the wheelchair. How do you think you would feel? How strong do you think your legs would be? After a year without working those muscles, your legs would look scrawny and be practically useless. You would probably have to learn how to walk again. That is the way that muscles work. If you do not work, move, and strengthen them, they will begin to become weak. In fact, a muscle can start to slowly die if it is not used for a long period of time.

In the same way, positivity is like a muscle. You must work it out. Instead of spending the year in a wheelchair, what if you used that year to work out your leg muscles every single day? After a year, they are going to look healthy and strong. Luckily, you will rid yourself of two toothpicks and replace them with two towering muscular legs like mine. Ha, ha, ha.

The method for building your physical muscles is the same for your positivity muscle. The more that you use your positivity muscle, the more positive you will become. The less that you use your positivity muscle, the less positive you will become.

How do you work out your positivity muscle? Well, just like jogging, lifting weights, playing sports and being active makes your muscles bigger, there is a workout that you can do with your positivity muscle. This workout is called gratitude.

That's right. Gratitude helps your positivity muscle grow stronger. On the other hand, if you are ungrateful, your positivity muscle will be small and weak. Let's be clear by getting a definition of gratitude. Gratitude is being thankful for where you are, what you have, and the people that are in your life right now.

When you are grateful, you rarely complain, are rarely sad, and completely avoid negativity. A grateful person looks for what is going well. Because of this, they can usually find positivity in situations that other people cannot.

A negative person reacts differently. For example, if their parent told them to take out the trash, they may think, "Why are my parents always bossing me around? Why do they always have to annoy me whenever I'm in the middle of something? Why can't they just take out the trash?" On the other hand, someone who uses their positivity muscle and is a grateful person would say, "You know what, I'm grateful for parents that try to teach me how important it is to work hard. I'm grateful for parents that are good, even if they ask me to do stuff that I don't want to do." A grateful person would say that their parents know what they're doing.

The gratitude method is extremely powerful. It is the number one way to build your positivity muscle. Why is it so important to be grateful? Just like you can't smile and be angry at the same time, you can't be negative and grateful at the same time. You can't feel blessed and stressed.

Did you know that one side of the brain activates gratitude and peace while the other side of the brain activates stress and sadness? Here is the catch, both sides of the brain can't operate at the same time. One must be active while the other stays inactive.

Literally and scientifically, you cannot feel blessed and stressed at the same time. This means that anytime you are in a state of gratitude, you are strengthening your positivity muscle, but anytime you're ungrateful, you're weakening that positivity muscle. Gratitude activates growth of the positivity muscle and strengthens a positive lifestyle.

Staying in a state of gratitude sounds great, but many people struggle with this. Well, gratitude is like perspective. The way we become grateful is by changing the way we view life's situations. Let me give you an example.

One day, my dad and I were jogging and there were dark clouds above us. It looked like it was about to storm, and my dad said, "Man, I really don't like gloomy days. I wish it was sunny." We continued to jog until we ended up going in the opposite direction. We couldn't believe our eyes. Once we changed directions, we saw the most beautiful sunset that we had ever seen in our entire lives. The clouds that were once blocking the sun, were now used to reflect the brightness of the sun.

We were both shocked, and my dad said, "A day that looked gloomy turned out to be one of the most beautiful days that I've ever seen." He then said, "Son, that's actually a good lesson. It's only a gloomy day if you look at the gloomy side, but if you change your view, you will see the beauty in the gloom."

This is a lesson for you as well. Instead of looking at the storm, turn your mindset around and look at the beautiful sunset. Instead of always looking at the negativity in your day, focus on positivity by finding things you can be grateful for.

Positivity will flow in your life when gratitude flows out of your heart. When you start looking at the good parts of your life, more good will come to you. Therefore, it is extremely important to start every day saying, "thank you." Constantly say, "Wow, thank you, God for giving me__________." (You can fill in the blank with something new every single day).

When you have something in your life that is going well, make sure that you say thank you. Say, "Thank you, God for the cool t-shirt in my closet. Thank you, God for allowing me to have a supportive family. Thank you, God for allowing me to live in a nice place." There is always something to be grateful for.

Saying, "thank you," to other people is just as important as your daily gratitude to God. When you're feeling gratitude towards someone, let them know. For example, I already know that most of you have a parents or guardian that has invested in you at some point in your life. Every kid doesn't have this blessing. You shouldn't just feel gratitude, but you should express this to your parents or guardian.

We are going to do this together. Pull out a piece of paper, and I want you to write a little thank you note to your parents. You don't just have to thank them for being your parents. You can thank them for their hard work and support. Also, you can thank them for a valuable lesson they taught you.

You don't need to wait for special moments to say, "thank you." Also, your thank you doesn't have to come with a present or a note. While you should make it a priority to use special moments for gratitude, you can make simple gratitude a daily, consistent practice. Find something to thank your parents for every day. When you go to a restaurant, thank your waiter or waitress. Classy people are thankful people. Kids that show gratitude are the ones that people like to be around. These kids have smiles on their faces and bring joy to others. No one likes to be around a kid that is selfish and ungrateful.

If you are struggling with gratitude, I'm going to share a strategy that really helped me work my positivity muscle and increase my gratitude. It is called a gratitude walk. Every morning before school, I would wake up and go for about a 10-minute walk. During that 10-minute walk, I would say things that I was grateful for. Not only would I say them to myself, but I would say them out loud. It may sound strange, but I would walk around my neighborhood saying, "Thank you for the awesome weather. Thank you that I have a teacher that supports me. Thank you that I'm athletic and am able to play sports." Every morning, I would practice simple gratitude and it changed my life. My day started with gratitude and continued throughout the day.

I made sure that gratitude was first so that I would not invite complaints into my day. Because I understood the importance of gratitude, I didn't start my day with video games or my phone, but I would focus on the things that I was grateful for.

Therefore, as positivity flowed out of my life, positivity flowed into my life. I'm going to challenge you guys to start taking gratitude walks. Tomorrow morning, wake up a little bit earlier and for 10 minutes, with your parents' permission, go on a gratitude walk. While you walk, say the things you are grateful for out loud.

Also, there were times that my dad and I would share our gratitude with one another. I would start by saying something I was grateful for and then my dad would do the same. We would do this for about 15 minutes. It was a great way to experience gratitude together. This is also something you can incorporate with your family or friends especially if you are feeling particularly negative. Sit down with your family or friends and share your gratitude with one another and watch the mood and energy in the room completely change.

It is important for you to remember that life is not always going to be good. There will be days that you will be disappointed, sad, frustrated, or depressed. This is normal. However, those are the moments that gratitude is especially useful. Despite your feelings or the situation, you must continue to work your gratitude muscle. Think about it this way. If I lift a 3-pound weight, it may only be a little challenging. However, if I lift a 78-pound weight, it is going to be a huge challenge. Even though the heavier one will be more challenging, it will produce greater results than the lighter one. The reason for this is that the more weight that you lift, the more your muscle will grow.

Similarly, when circumstances are easy, it's like that 3-pound weight. Anybody can be grateful when life is going well. But when life is difficult, that is when gratitude can have the greatest results. That is when the positivity muscle will truly grow.

Don't wait for the right circumstances to cause you to be grateful. When you're not feeling good, that is the perfect time to be grateful. Remember, your life doesn't get good then you get grateful. You get grateful and then your life will get good. Now, join the gratitude gym and work your positivity muscle until you come out looking like Arnold Schwarzenegger.

4

Watch Your Words

Let's start this chapter with a game. Here is how it works. I'm going to give you a scenario and two separate responses to the scenario. Then, you're going to tell me which response is more positive. You ready? Okay. Let's do it.

Scenario 1:

Jerry was at a theme park. The line was long, and it was unbelievably hot outside. Jerry said, "Oh, I hate long lines. Why does this always have to happen to me? The roller coaster probably won't even be worth it. This is going to take forever, and it's way too hot. Look at me. I'm pouring sweat. This is disgusting."

Judy was at the same theme park, and she was experiencing the same conditions. Judy said, "It may be a long line, but at least it gives me some time to think about my goals. Hey, you never know. Maybe I'll meet a friend. Also, I know this roller coaster is going to be well worth the wait. It's going to be a lot of fun. I love the feeling that roller coasters give my stomach whenever there is a large drop. The heat is causing me to sweat, but I heard that sweating is good for my body. It's supposed to make my skin clearer."

Who do you think was more positive? Who do you think was more negative? Who do you think had a better day at the theme park? If you said that Judy was the more positive person, then you are correct. Of course, she's the positive one, and Jerry is the negative one.

Here's the winning question. How did you know who was the more positive person? If you said you identified the positive person because of what they said about their situation, then you are a winner. You don't know anything about Jerry or Judy. You don't know their parents or where they go to school. I didn't even tell you how old they are. When it comes to positivity, none of this information matters. Another important identifying habit of a positive person is the words they speak. The same can be said for a negative person. There are specific words they use in reaction to circumstances that identify them as a positive or negative person.

Years ago, I started to understand the connection between my words and a positive attitude. I was on my way to baseball practice, and that day, I really did not want to go. I was feeling sore, and I knew we weren't going to be doing anything I enjoyed. It was one of those baseball practices where we focused on exercise and drills. I spent the day at school telling my friends, "I really don't want to go to baseball practice today. It is not going to be fun at all."

My dad picked me up after school and the first thing I said when I got in the car was, "Dad, why do we have to go today?" My dad looked at me, but he did not respond. I was a little bit confused, but I did not ask him the question again. When we arrived at practice, I had a bad attitude from start to finish. It was boring, I was feeling sore, and I wasn't playing well at all. I couldn't hit right, and I was missing all the ground and fly balls.

Devastated by my performance, I went home after practice and complained for at least 30 minutes. I said, "Man, I hate baseball practice. I hate the drills and workouts. It is so boring, and it doesn't really help me become a better player."

The next week, I had that familiar feeling of dread. I didn't want to go to practice again. When I got into the back of the car, I said, "Man, why do we have to go to baseball practice?" My dad looked at me, and said, "Last week, I let it slide, because I wanted you to realize what happens when you act like you have to do something. This week, I want to teach you a valuable lesson. You need to turn your have to's into get to's."

I said, "What do you mean by that?" He said, "Well, the words you say are important. Because you went into practice saying it was going to be boring and that you were going to hate the workouts and drills, it ended up being bad. However, if you went into that practice saying, 'Yes, I get to go to baseball practice. Look at how awesome it is. There are some people who aren't able play baseball, but I am able to play. There are some people who don't have legs. There are some kids who are in hospitals because they're sick. I get to practice so that I can perform better." Then, my dad said, "You looked at all the negative things, and more importantly, *said* all of the negative things. That's why it was awful."

He said, "What I want you to do right now is to say, 'Yes, I get to go to baseball practice.' Once you've completed this, I want you to say why this practice is going to be awesome."

I said, "Okay. I get to go to baseball practice, and it's awesome because I'm going to become a better player because of it." He said, 'Okay, that's good. Say another one." I said, "I get to go to baseball practice and it's going to be fun because I'm going to get to hang out with all my friends." He said, "That's good. Say another one."

I said, "I get to go to baseball practice and it's going to be fun because I get to run around when there are some kids that are physically unable to do this." He said, "Okay, say another one." I said, "I get to go to baseball practice, and it's going to be fun because I am able to play baseball when most of my friends' parents won't let them play sports."

This happened until I arrived at baseball practice. When I was about to step out on the field, I noticed that I felt completely different at this week's practice. I thought, "Man, my dad's right. I am blessed, and this is going to be a lot of fun." I went out on the field and had one of my best practices. I felt mentally and physically energized, and the next week I did the same thing.

On the way to every practice, I said positive statements. From that point forward, I made positive, "get to's," a habit. Because of this, I felt positive before and after every baseball practice, which made a huge difference.

That was such a powerful lesson my dad taught me. Baseball practice never changed, but what I was saying about it did change. As my words changed, my attitude changed. This lesson can be applied to anything in your life. There are so many times we use negative words to react to our lives. As I said before, when you change your perspective, you are able to see the positive even if you are in a negative situation.

Not only should you change your perspective, but you must focus on saying positive words. Positive words bring positive results. One way to do this is to start turning your, "have to's" into "get to's." Instead of saying, "I have to take this test, and it's going to be hard," say, "I get to take this test, and it is going to increase my knowledge and prepare me for other life's challenges."

Instead of saying, "I have to hang out with this person, and I don't really have fun with them," say, "I get to hang out with this person, and I'm going to have fun and smile."

It can be difficult to change your negative talk into positive talk. To help you make positive talk a habit, try to monitor your words. One thing that I used to do is wear a bracelet or a rubber band around my left wrist. Any time I caught myself saying something negative, I would lightly snap it on myself. It wouldn't hurt, but it would alert me to my negative words. After I recognized the negative words, I would switch them into positive words.

This is something that I encourage you guys to do. Start wearing a rubber band, wrist band or something similar. Any time you catch yourself saying something negative, quickly snap yourself. Once again, don't hurt yourself. Lightly pull the object around your wrist so you can recognize your negativity. Then, say something positive. After doing this for a short time, you're no longer going to be saying negative words.

Not only should you be turning your, "have tos" into "get tos," you should be turning your complaints into solutions. I've learned that words that don't get something done are wasted. If you say, "Oh, man, my bike isn't working," literally, nothing changed with your bike. I call these, gate statements because they stop you from moving forward with a solution. If you were to say, "Oh, man, my bike's not working. What can I do to fix it," then your brain starts to look for creative solutions. I call these growth statements. It's important that you use growth statements to ignite creative solutions instead of making gate statements that simply state the obvious.

For example, if you say, "I'm so frustrated that I don't have any money," it automatically freezes your mindset and makes you believe that you are in this permanent state. The problem with this statement is that there is nothing else that you can say. If you say, "Hey, right now I might not have any money, but I can think of ways to make money," your brain is going to automatically strategize. The second statement motivates creative thinking while the first is a statement of fact without a solution. Instead of complaining and wasting your words, turn them into solutions.

We've talked about two main strategies for improving your words so that you can be a positive kid. Number one, start saying, "get to," instead of, "have to." Number two, start looking for solutions rather than complaints. The third strategy is to start viewing challenges as opportunities. You must become what I like to call, reverse paranoid. Okay, you're probably thinking, "Whoa, Caleb. Those are some big words right there."

Let me simplify it. Have you ever heard of someone being paranoid? Paranoid means that someone is always scared that something bad is going to happen in the future. They may be worried that someone's going to hack into their phone; jump out of an alley and hurt them; their boss is going to fire them; or they are going to fail their assignments. Paranoid people are constantly worried about negative situations that could happen.

Even when there's not a problem, they look for problems. Instead of being paranoid, try to become reverse paranoid. What do I mean by that? Always focus on the good that could happen in every future situation. Think about the ways the world is working for you rather than believing that the world is out to get you.

Let's say that you think one of your friends is talking about you at school, but you're not exactly sure. Don't be paranoid and think, "Oh, she is gossiping and saying mean things about me." Start thinking, "Well, she may be saying nice things about me, or she may not be talking about me at all."

If you believe your coach is about to cut you from the team, start thinking, "What if my coach promotes me?" Becoming reverse paranoid will allow you to see how life is working for you. If you break your phone, say, "Well, maybe when I get it fixed, I will meet someone that is going to help me in my future. I might even meet a new friend."

Even when the situation seems terrible, look for possible positive outcomes. For example, the other day, my mom left her laptop on top of her car and drove away. It fell off her car, and it was immediately destroyed. At first, my mom was devastated and started looking at all the things that were going to go wrong because her computer broke. She started thinking about the files she lost, the amount of money she paid for the computer, and the cost for a replacement. I could see that she was becoming paranoid, and it was affecting her. Before she allowed these thoughts to grow, she caught herself. I was so proud of her.

She stopped thinking about all the negative that could come from this situation and became reverse paranoid. She looked at how breaking her laptop could be a benefit. She started thinking, "Well, maybe there is someone that could help me pay for it. I might even be able to get a better laptop and meet someone new in the process."

She focused her thoughts and energy on the positive results that could come. Guess what? Shortly after, someone bought her a better laptop, so she was able to get an upgrade for free.

Becoming reverse paranoid will reduce the amount of worry and anxiety that many people experience daily. There is no need to worry about the future because in most situations, you cannot control it. However, you can control the way you view it. Don't allow fear and negative thoughts to overcome your mind. In every situation, think about the best possible outcome, and you will experience a more positive outlook.

Using these three strategies will allow you to use your words to build your positivity muscle. You are well on your way to becoming one of the most positive kids on the planet. Let's keep reading.

5

Dealing with Negative Friends and Family

Have you ever heard the phrase, "Guilty by association?" This phrase means that even if you haven't done anything wrong, the people that you surround yourself with can either help or harm you. The people you spend the most time with will determine if you are going to be a positive or negative person.

This is an important principle to master because if you don't get this one, then the other chapters won't be as useful to you. Relationships play a huge role in our lives. In fact, you can do everything that this book tells you to do, but the negative family and friends you keep close to you will cause you to become negative as well. Negative people like to be around others that are negative. The same is true for positive people.

For example, when I was about 11 years old, I really felt as though I had a strong positive attitude. I was reverse paranoid, used positive words, and smiled when I felt negative. Also, I was in control of my attitude and worked out my positivity muscle daily.

Then, I started hanging around a guy in school that was negative. He wasn't a bad person, but his attitude was poor. If something happened, he would always look for the negative while I looked for the good. I noticed his negative habits right away, but I thought that if he was around me, I would rub off on him and make him more positive.

In reality, I learned that most of the time, the negative will overcome the positive instead of the other way around. The more time I spent with him, the more I started catching myself saying negative things. It felt like I was going backwards on my positive journey. That's something you always want to look out for on your overall success journey.

Never be in a state of going backwards but always be going forward.

My dad noticed the shift in my attitude. Because he didn't know my friend well, he didn't realize that my change was due to this friendship. In response to my attitude, he would say, "Dude. What's wrong with you? You're saying a lot of negative stuff. You seem less happy than you were before."

I kept spending a good deal of time with my friend because I didn't realize that my negative attitude was connected to this friendship. For a couple weeks, I struggled with my moods, attitude, and behavior. I was upset all the time and became sad easily. Finally, I couldn't take it anymore. I said, "What is wrong? I don't know why I'm not being positive. I feel so negative right now. I don't know what's going on. How can I fix this?" I felt stuck.

My answers came around the time my friend went on vacation for two weeks. When he was gone, I felt like myself again. I started becoming more positive, my mood improved, and my natural smile returned.

When he came back, that familiar negativity crept back in. I started to realize that this friendship was the root of my negativity. Now, you always want to take responsibility for your behaviors, but you also want to be mindful of the fact that people do play a major role in your positivity. Friends, and more importantly family, make an extreme difference in your life. When you are aware of this, you can be more strategic with the friends and family members you allow to become close to you.

If you have a negative close friend, there are three steps to deal with them effectively.

The first step in dealing with a negative friend is to either end the friendship or limit your time spent with that person. This may be difficult because many times, you make a connection with someone even if they are negative. You may see the good in this person. You may have a lot in common with them. You may even see great potential within them. The truth that you must understand is that there are many sacrifices you must make on your road to success. Everyone is not meant to come with you on your journey and that is ok.

I didn't completely end my friendship because I didn't want to be rude by just stopping all communication. Instead, I limited the amount of time I spent with him. We would hang out once a week, as opposed to every day. Eventually, we only hung out once every three weeks.

Friends like these are just like cheat meals with your health. It's okay to occasionally have a burger, but if you have a burger every day, your health is going to suffer. It's the exact same way with your friends. Even though some of your friends are fun to be around, they may become harmful to you. They are good now and then, but if you're around them all the time, it will start to mentally and emotionally harm you. Therefore, it is important for you to limit the time that you spend with some of these friends.

I want you to identify some of your friends that are negative. Think about the friends that you should probably limit your time with. Once you know who these friends are, start limiting the time you spend with them. Also, another way to deal with negative friendships, is to make sure that you have positive friends. As important as it is to get rid of the negative ones, it's as important to get positive ones. Identify your positive friends and start spending more time with them.

You can also use the limited time you spend with your negative friend as an opportunity to share your positive journey. A great way to do this is to invite them to read this book with you. As you read together, you can discuss the topics and hold each other accountable to apply what you are learning. Start getting your friends involved in your success journey, so they can become successful as well.

The second step in dealing with negative friends is to share the information you've learned about positivity. It would also be helpful for you to discuss the impact of their negativity. You should be honest with your friend and tell them about how their negativity will affect them and the people that are close to them. This is one thing that I did with my friend. I told him, "Hey man. I really enjoy hanging out with you. You're a cool guy. We have fun, but honestly, I have some really big goals that require a positive attitude to achieve them." I then told him that his negative attitude was affecting me.

I did not share this information with my friend because I was trying to change him. The reality is, there are some friends you can never change. They are who they are. Then there are some friends that are willing to change, but it must be their decision. Your responsibility is to simply share the information. They must make the decision to change. They may have never heard about the power of positivity before. You can be that person that tells them.

I not only wanted to tell my friend about his negativity, but I also wanted to provide some resources that would help him gain a more positive attitude. I gave him some success books and my friend started reading them. He became a little better. Even though he improved, I still couldn't spend a lot of time with him, but the time we did spend together was more productive because we shared a similar mindset.

As you continue to share what you are learning, you will begin to create a close circle of friends that are positive and focused.

I heard from one kid that said he started reading my books with eight of his friends at school. Every week, they would meet up and talk about the book and a video that I posted on social media. They shared what they were learning and the way they were applying the information. Because of the support from each other, this group is excelling. They are becoming successful kids because they are encouraging each other through the process.

The third step in dealing with negative friends is to have more positivity than they have negativity. One of my favorite sayings is, "You can't keep a bird from flying over your head, but you can keep it from making a nest in your hair."

What does that have to do with negative friends? Well that means you can't stop some of your friends from being negative, but you can stop them from making you negative. You can overcome their negativity with your positivity. If you hear your friend say, "This thing is so expensive. I hate when I don't have the money to buy what I want." You can speak up and say, "Yeah, but it's not too expensive.

You know, when we become successful we will have more than enough money to buy it."

One of your friends may earn a bad grade on their test and say, "Why is the teacher so unfair? I'm never going to get a good grade in this class." You can be even more positive and say, "Yeah, but a bad grade can help you learn how to study better. We can make a list of ways to study that will help you get a better grade on the next test."

If your friend is more negative than you are positive, then you are going to be more negative. The opposite is also true. If you are more positive than you friend is negative, then you will keep your surroundings positive. Make sure to be at least 3 times more positive than others are negative. For every complaint they say, you come up with at least three positive solutions.

Sometimes, despite your best efforts, your friends may remain negative. In that case, you must make the hard decision of removing them for your life so that others can come in that will be a benefit you. You must protect your inner circle. This means that the people close to you should be positive kids that are focused on growing and learning.

Remember, a boat never sinks from the water outside of it. It only sinks from the water inside of it. Imagine that you are the boat and the water that is surrounding you is people. These can be the people that you see every day, but you aren't necessarily close to them. The people on the inside of the boat would be your closest friends. These are the people that you spend the most time with and have the greatest influence in your life. The people that may hold you back or harm your success will be those closest to you. This is why you must choose your friends wisely so that the ones that are closest to you are always encouraging and challenging you to become better.

While you have control over who your friends are, you are not able to choose your family. With negative friends, you can decide to no longer spend time with them, but when it comes to family, you don't have a choice. Dealing with negative family members can be a little more difficult. I can personally relate to this because I have multiple negative family members.

You can use similar steps in dealing with negative family members that you used when dealing with negative friends. However, you should never cut off a family member. The relationships you have with your family are important, so do whatever you have to do to keep building them.

Living with negative family members can be challenging. It is not you job to change them, but it is your job to make sure that you maintain a healthy mindset and positive attitude. There are times when you may need to leave the room, go on a walk, or shift your mind to something else. The most important thing to remember is to not focus on their negativity. This will drain you, so protect your energy and come up with unique ways to escape their negativity.

You have the power over your own mind and energy, which means that you must decide to not allow that negative energy into your space. If you are with a family member and they become negative, your enthusiasm can defeat their negativity.

One way that I have dealt with negative family members is to go to another room and make a list of

10 things that I am grateful for. Also, I go into another room and play music or start singing my favorite song. The key to dealing with family members is maintaining a positive attitude. Remember, it is not your job to try and change your negative family members. Your job is to remain positive and protect your mindset.

Dealing with negative friends and family members can be tough, but it is possible to overcome that negative energy. Through the negativity of those close to me, I've been able to strengthen my positive muscle. Use these relationships as challenges to become a stronger, more positive kid. I believe in you!

6

What you Put in is What You Get Out

Throughout this book, you learned about the importance of your mindset and what you put out into the environment. Think about it. We talked about making the choice to be positive, going the extra smile, living a life of gratitude, speaking positive words, and dealing with negative family members. Everything that we have gone over thus far has focused on what you are putting out into the world. Although it is extremely important to focus on what you put out, it is also extremely important to watch what you put in.

In other words, what you put in your body and mind will affect what you put out. If you're constantly putting in negative thoughts, watching negative shows, listening to negative music, and eating unhealthy foods, then it will be difficult to put out positivity. This is because you are filled with negativity, and what is on the inside will flow to the outside. There are three main things that you put into your body that can directly affect your attitude.

The first thing is the foods you eat. I know you guys have heard me say this a lot but foods really do affect moods. When I was younger, I used to play a lot of baseball. That's not anything new to you guys. You can obviously tell by the stories I've shared in this book that baseball used to be a major part of my life. The days we were scheduled to play tournaments were long and exhausting. We would spend hours in the sun and play back to back games until it was over. The heat and hard work made it easy to lose energy, feel negative and become moody. In order to combat that, all my friends including me, used to do the craziest things to try to stay energized.

One way we would try to stay mentally tough and energetic is to eat snacks from the concession stand and stay hydrated. Gatorade was the drink of choice for most of my friends. I used to drink it all the time as well. Even though it tasted good, I remember feeling sluggish after I drank one. Not only did I drink Gatorade, but I also drank sodas because they were available during the games. During some of our breaks, my friends and I would go to the concession stand and eat burgers and hotdogs.

That all changed when I asked my dad why I felt like I was losing a great deal of energy during the games. My dad told me that statement I use all the time. "Foods affect moods." I asked him what he meant by that. He's said, "What you put in is what you get out." I responded by saying, "Dad, these are some great quotes to put on Twitter, but can you tell me what you are talking about?" He laughed and said, "Caleb, think about the things that you ate today since we started playing baseball. You had a cheeseburger, a hot dog, French fries, a whole bunch of Gatorade and a little bit of soda." He said, "With all of that unhealthy stuff that's in your body, how do you expect to stay energetic? How do you expect to keep a positive mental attitude?"

My dad's explanation made a lot of sense, so I asked him what he thought I should be eating and drinking. He said, "You know what, I know we're playing today and we have one more game. Let's just push through today's game and we will change your food and drink choices for tomorrow. I'm going to get you drinks and food that will help your mood and energy." I agreed to his plan and was excited about the results.

The next morning, I woke up and my dad had already been up for about 30 minutes preparing my food and drinks. The first thing he had was a whole gallon filled with water and freshly squeezed lemons. He said, "Caleb, instead of drinking Gatorade, you're going to drink this." I said, "Dad, isn't Gatorade supposed to be super healthy? That is what they always say."

He said, "Even though there may be some small benefits of drinking Gatorade, it's also packed with sugar. It's important that you replace sugary drinks and soda with water." "What are the benefits of drinking water with lemon?" I asked. He said, "When you drink water with lemon, you will have more energy and healthier skin." Not only did my dad prepare drinks for me, but he also had food as well. There was a bowl of fruit, two bananas, and two fresh fruit juices. My dad told me that I was going to eat and drink these items throughout the day.

We got to the baseball field, and all my friends were already drinking Gatorade. I really liked Gatorade so at first the different flavors looked good. Then I thought, I may crave a Gatorade right now, but I'm going to make a sacrifice now so that I can keep high energy throughout the day.

Unlike my friends, I drank water while they chugged their Gatorade. Within an hour, I had an incredible amount of energy. At the same time, I noticed that some of my friends were already looking sluggish. I could tell that the simple change to water was already working. After the first game was played, all my friends headed over to the concession stand to get a burger and hotdog. This was our tradition after every first game.

While my friends ate their food from the concession stand, I had a bowl of fresh fruit. When it was time for the second game to start, I was still filled with energy. I had more energy at that moment than I did before the start of the first game. My teammates seemed to struggle. They were playing slower and had more errors. The strange part was that I started having one of my best games ever. I hit better because I felt extra light and fast. I was diving for balls, throwing faster, and running harder than my teammates.

By the time the day was over, I could have played a couple more games. My teammates appeared to be exhausted and weak. When we got home that night, my dad brought up the lesson he taught me the night before. He said, "Caleb, remember. Foods affect moods. This means that foods are going to affect your positivity, what you say, and how you feel." From that day forward, I continued to make healthier food and drink choices.

My choice to become healthier made an impression on others. Umpires and professional baseball scouts noticed the difference in my energy as compared to the other players. My teammates noticed the change as well, and as a team, we made healthier choices before, during, and after games. The result was that we were more positive, energetic and more importantly, we were having more fun because our attitudes remained positive.

As I stated earlier, you should be aware of what you are putting in your body. There are a couple of things I want to encourage you guys to start doing to become more positive. The first change that I want you guys to make is to drink water with lemons instead of soda or other sugary drinks. Water with lemons is going to make an enormous difference in your life. You're going to feel better than you've ever felt. If you make this simple change, you're going to be healthier, live longer, be more energetic, and have clearer skin. Those other drinks may look better or taste better, but the health benefits you receive from water with lemon will make you *feel* better.

Try to drink only one soda per week. I made this change not only for baseball, but I do it for my every day health. For every time you drink soda, I want you to replace it with water with lemons. If you drink 2 sodas a day, then replace those with 2 glasses of water with lemon. Let's be the healthiest kids on the planet, and that starts with staying hydrated with the best liquid that will give you the greatest benefits.

The second change I want you to make is the foods that you're putting into your body. If you are reading this book, you must become health-conscious. That simply means that you will start thinking about and taking care of your health. I know this is not a book about health but about positivity. However, foods are closely connected to positivity. In fact, I believe that one of the main reasons people are negative is based on what they eat.

I have a family member that is overweight. He spends most of his time eating unhealthy foods. The result of this is a negative attitude. One day, I asked him, "Why are you so negative." He responded by stating, "One of the main reasons that I'm negative is because I am overweight. I've been bullied by others, and I have no energy. There are some changes I want to make, but I just don't know where to start. I don't want to be sad or upset every day, but I feel like I can't control my cravings for unhealthy food and drinks."

I asked him what he normally eats. He listed foods such as cheeseburgers, fried chicken, chips, pizza, fries, soda, etc. I knew that these foods were affecting his moods. I shared with my family member the information I'm sharing with you in this book. I told him that he needed to start eating healthier foods like organic rice, organic chicken, fruits and vegetables.

Then, I challenged him to change his diet to these types of foods for a week and keep track of his moods and energy levels. I'm sure this is not a surprise to you, but after a week, my family member said he felt better than he had in a long time. He said that his energy level was high every day, he smiled easily, and he felt better after he finished his meals. After 3 days, he even started going on walks.

Most of you are already aware of the way your food affects your moods. Have you ever had a ton of pizza and started to feel greasy, bloated, tired, and moody throughout the day? That food may bring temporary happiness because it tastes good at the time. The only problem is that this temporary pleasure only lasts while you are eating it. The negative affects you feel after finishing the food are not worth it. That is because the food that you put in your body makes a huge difference in how you feel after you eat it.

You will find that after you eat a good amount of fruit or vegetables, you feel energetic and happy. Now, I'm not telling you to never eat cheeseburgers, pizza, desserts, or soda. Just make sure that you limit the amount of these foods that you eat. Be the kid at a restaurant that orders a salad while the rest of your friends fill their bodies with greasy pizza or burgers.

Don't fall into the limiting beliefs about health foods. Vegetables and anything green do not taste disgusting. I'll let you in on a secret. I think that healthier food tastes better than unhealthy food. Like any change you make, your body will have to get used to it. When you make healthy eating a habit, you will find that your body no longer craves unhealthy food. Instead, your body will begin to crave fruits, vegetables, organic meats, and water with lemon. I know this sounds crazy, but guys, it is true.

The third change you need to make is what you watch and listen to. There are so many options for entertainment such as YouTube videos, Hulu, Netflix, and shows on live television. Watching movies and TV shows can be fun and relaxing. However, the content in most of these shows can be negative. The kids in some of the shows are disrespectful to their parents, making poor life choices, bullying, doing drugs, or involved in suicide. Not only that, watching TV or movies can become addicting. Sitting in front of a screen all day can make you just as tired and sluggish as eating unhealthy food.

The images that you are watching all day will have an impact on you. If all the TV shows and movies you watch have cursing, violence, and inappropriate activities, they will start to impact your moods and behaviors. You don't have to cut out entertainment completely. Schedule weekly relaxation time that includes watching TV or a movie. Try to pick something with a positive message and images that encourage your journey towards success.

The same thing can be said about music. It is available everywhere. Music can be used to elevate moods and energy, and there is a wide variety to choose from. It is important for you to be responsible in your choice of music. The words that are sung are more important than you realize. If you are spending your day listening to music with negative lyrics that contain cursing, disrespect to authority, and sex, it will eventually effect the way you think and act.

I can prove it. When you go to the gym, I guarantee that you will see people with headphones on listening to music. Most of the time, they are listening to upbeat music because it elevates their energy. If you go to the doctor's or dentist's office, there is relaxing music played quietly in the waiting room to set a calm atmosphere. Music is powerful and can have a huge impact on your moods, behavior, and words.

Watch and listen to things that help you grow. There are two categories of entertainment. The first category is called, gate entertainment. The second category is called, growth entertainment. Gate entertainment does nothing but stop you. It literally brings you to a complete halt. This means that when you watch a show on Nickelodeon, it may not harm you, but it doesn't do much to help you grow or become a more successful kid.

If you're watching shows every day that are purely entertaining, it becomes a waste of 23 minutes. Gate entertainment can come in many forms, but it includes shows and music that can be used as an escape from reality. It doesn't help you grow or add value to your life. This category of entertainment should only be used 2-3 times per week.

Growth entertainment should be enjoyed at least once a day. A perfect example of growth entertainment would be reading my books and watching my videos. They are fun and help you learn all at the same time. You may learn something that is going to change your life and help you get results. Choose more growth entertainment options that will keep you focused and give you useful information that will help you become successful. Remember, pay attention to what you're watching and listening to.

The third change is to spend your time wisely. I constantly see kids spend their free time playing video games, texting their friends, scrolling through social media, or laying around and doing nothing. As important as it is to watch your words, it's 10 times more important to watch your actions. You may not understand this now, but what you do today will determine who you become tomorrow.

Instead of playing video games, substitute them with reading a success book. That is an action that will help you grow. Instead of gossiping on the phone with your friends, talk about success strategies or ideas for a business. Instead of scrolling through Facebook, spend some time meeting and talking to other successful kids.

Once again, I'm not saying that you can't relax and have fun. Just make sure to do everything in moderation, which means that you shouldn't over do anything. If you play video games every day for 2 hours, try to do it in moderation by playing every other day for 30 minutes.

Be intentional about what you eat, listen to, watch, and do. These parts of your life help you put positivity in and put positivity out. This combination will help you have an unstoppable positive attitude.

7

What to do When Nothing is Going Good

Wow! You almost have every necessary tool to become the most positive kid in the world. If you apply the information I've given in this book, you will see results. Not only that, the people close to you will be able to tell the difference as well. Before we end this book, I want to share one more bit of information with you. If you have been a Maddix Addict for any amount of time, this information will be familiar to you because I talk about it all the time. Let's get into it, guys.

We've spent a good amount of time going over how important it is to be positive, but there are going to be moments when you feel like nothing is going right for you. You might have one of those weeks where you feel like everything and everyone is against you. Trust me, I've been there. I had one memorable week that was so upsetting, I felt like I was falling in an endless pit of negativity. I was having family problems, my business was struggling, I couldn't close any sales, and I was ending each day with an overall sense of defeat.

Not only that, I wasn't feeling well. It felt like I was on this side of negativity and positivity was on the other side of a six-foot-wide brick wall. All I could do was keep running into the wall in hopes that I would finally break through, but it wasn't happening. Nothing was breaking through or going right, so I thought that the problem was I wasn't working hard enough. I decided to work harder which included smiling more, gratitude walks, healthy eating, and growth entertainment.

Working harder left me frustrated and tired. Finally, I realized that I may be focusing too much on myself. One morning, I woke up and even though I still wasn't feeling well, I decided to go and do something nice for someone.

The first thing that I did was purchase sleeping bags, and I gave them to some homeless people. After that, I started to feel a little bit better. Next, I gave a $100 bill to a struggling single mother. After I gave her the money, she started crying. She said, "I didn't know how I was going to feed my kids this week. This gift makes it possible. Thank you so much." I also gave a bike to a fatherless kid and spent time encouraging some of my friends that were having a rough time.

I challenged myself to give as much as I possibly could. It didn't cause an automatic transformation, but I started to feel more fulfilled and positive.

Later on that week, I received a notification from a guy from Australia. Before I tell you what he said, it's important that you know that I write all my goals daily. One of my goals was to speak with a guy named Gary Vaynerchuk. I wrote it every single day for about a year and a half. "I will speak with Gary Vaynerchuk." Despite my goal, nothing seemed to be happening to fulfill it.

This Australian guy was an event planner. He said, "Good day, mate. I have a question for you. I do some events in Australia and I would like for you to speak at one of them. There's going to be about 600 business people and real estate agents at the event. One of the speakers will be Gary Vaynerchuk. Would you be interested in speaking?" When I heard that message, I was blown away.

That week, despite my best efforts, I had not received any speaking requests. I couldn't seem to escape my negative funk, and nothing seemed to be going right. But the moment I put impact over income, was the moment that a life changing opportunity came.

This taught me such a valuable lesson. When nothing is going good for you, do something good for somebody else. After that, opportunities continued to arise, and I knew that I had to add an extra positivity technique to my arsenal. Giving back is the last key to positivity.

When life is not going well, you're feeling disappointed, something unfair happens, or you are becoming negative, overcome it with giving back. Don't just give when you're not feeling good, but give when you feel the best because you will feel even better. Not only that, but you will make a difference.

You don't have to buy something or give money away to make a difference in someone's life. I am fortunate enough to have the ability to use some of the money I make to give back to others, but that is not the only way I give back.

The first way that you can give back is to look at some of the stuff that you have. Many times, we have clothes, toys, books, games, blankets, stuffed animals, shoes etc. that we are no longer using. If your room is filled with some of these things that you no longer use, consider donating them to charity. These items will then be able to be used by someone in need.

Some of the greatest people in the world are currently homeless. They are not bad people, they are just in an unfortunate situation. These people usually have many needs. I used to have this favorite blanket that I had since I was a baby. One day, I told my dad that I wanted to take my blanket to a homeless person. I figured that there was someone that had to sleep outside and may be cold at night.

My dad took me to a homeless shelter where I gave my blanket to a young man in need. He was so grateful, and we were able to sit and talk with him.

I want you to look around your room. What are some things that you have that a homeless person could use? Ask your parents to help you with this. As a family, you can make a list of items that you can give away and even some that you can buy for the homeless. Some of the items you purchase can be as simple as soap, shampoo, deodorant, and a toothbrush.

You can also give homeless people food. Every Friday morning, my dad and I would give away coffee and donuts or pizza to the homeless. We would travel to the nearest homeless shelter and deliver the food items. While we were passing out the food, we would shake hands, hug, and speak with the homeless people. That is another way to give back as well. Kindness and compassion is so important. Connecting to other people can benefit you as well as the other person. This is something that is really going to make an impact on them.

Sometimes homeless people just want to talk, so maybe you could think of conversation starters and speak with them. Make sure that you involve your parents in each part of this. Do not go to a shelter by yourself or have conversations with strangers by yourself. Always go with an adult you know and trust.

Many times, there are people that we know that are in need as well. Kids we go to school with every day may need an encouraging word, a smile, or a friend. I used to have a classmate that would always sit alone during lunch. For the first month of school, I watched as he ate his lunch by himself. I felt bad, but at the same time I thought that there was nothing I could do. Luckily, I was positive, enthusiastic, and friendly so a lot of kids looked up to me. During lunch, I sat at a table with other kids that were considered the, "popular crowd."

After seeing this kid sit by himself for a month, I decided that if this was what being cool was, I didn't want to be cool. I would rather make a difference. But to make a difference, I knew I needed to be different.

I went to his lunch table and sat down by him. We hit it off immediately because he was a great kid, and we had a lot in common. The next day, one of my other friends said, "I'm going to go sit at the other table with Caleb." Soon, the entire table filled up with my friends. A table that used to have just one lonely kid, was now filled with the popular kids.

The great part about this was that we started bringing this positive energy into our classroom. Everyone began showing each other kindness and compassion. Our classroom was filled with positivity and there were no longer the separated groups of "popular kids" or "loners." We were all classmates and looked out for each other.

Simply showing someone kindness made a huge difference in our class. When you go to school tomorrow, start looking around for kids that may need some encouragement or a kind word. There are some kids that are looking for a friend or a nice conversation. Kindness and conversation will not cost you any money, and it will make a huge difference.

Also, strive to be the kid that compliments. Don't give insincere compliments, but if you see something that you admire, give a compliment. For instance, if one of your friends gets a new outfit or pair of shoes that you like, compliment them. If you see your friend show kindness to someone or do a great job on an assignment, give them a compliment. You can make someone feel good by giving them sincere compliments.

Kids at school and homeless people are not the only ones that we can give back to. There are also older people in nursing homes that may need some positive energy and encouragement. My parents and I would go to nursing homes to visit the elderly. Before we went, they would call and ask if I could give away some flowers and speak to the patients.

When we arrived, I would go into the rooms and spend time with some of the patients. I would encourage them, ask for their best advice, and give them flowers. They would all feel extremely blessed that I was there, and I also felt great that I was able to give back.

Another thing you can do is go to hospitals. My dad used to take me to the kids' cancer centers where there were kids the exact same age that I was that had cancer. I would talk with them, play video games, and hang out.

Another thing that you can do is go to the grocery store and carry people's groceries for them. My dad used to take me to the grocery store and any person I would see with a lot of bags, I would ask, "Hey, do you mind if I carry your groceries to the car?" It was just a simple act to make their day. You never know how much that will impact someone's life.

You can also send cards to people who are in need overseas or in another state. There are multiple organizations that can help you do this. Send cards to people to show your appreciation and gratitude. These cards can be sent to people you know like your grandparents, friends, or other relatives. Also, you can send cards to people in hospitals or the military.

This chapter supplied you with giving strategies. Now, it's your turn. The great part about being a leader is that you guys are smart. There are many different talents that you have and things that you can do to make a difference. I want you to make a list of the ways that you are going to give back. I want you to become a giver because I believe that when nothing is going good for you, you can do something good for somebody else. That is the model I want you to live by. Put your impact before your income. Put serving before selling. Put giving before everything else, and you will live a positive life.

For the next month, focus on applying this information so that you can become the most positive kid on the planet. Let's keep growing and progressing as we become better leaders, givers, and world changers.

Message from Matt to the Parents

Listen, parents. This could be the most important book that your kids read because if they can master their attitude, they can master anything in life. Attitude literally determines everything. I'm going to give you some practical strategies to ensure that you lead your kids into a positive lifestyle, mindset, and energy.

Over the years, one of the most important lessons that I've learned is that a positive attitude begins with the right mindset. There are two secrets to acquiring the right mindset, and the first secret is to always have the right perspective.

Let's say that your kid forgets to take his lunchbox to school. You are obviously going to be frustrated or upset. You have every right to be. It is important for our kids to learn responsibility. I also understand the importance of punishments and consequences. However, don't forget to put things in proper perspective. Correct your kids when they do wrong, but don't berate them with negative language.

There are many times that situations will be out of our control. We may become frustrated, upset, or angry. In those moments, remember that we are the leaders that must continue to show our kids the value of keeping things in the right perspective. Yes, your kid may have forgot his lunchbox, but he is still alive and safe. A proper perspective would see this as an opportunity for your child to write a list of ways that he can become more responsible.

Even though Caleb went through some difficulty as a kid, one of the main motivators that kept him focused and positive was responding to life with the right perspective. This skill did not come naturally. I made sure to model this behavior every time the opportunity presented itself.

Some of you that are reading this book may be divorced and are raising your kids as a single parent. I can relate. Caleb's mom and I divorced when he was

4 years old. This meant that he had to go back and forth between houses at a very young age. At first, the adjustment was hard on all of us.

I couldn't do anything to change the situation because it was a reality. However, I consistently helped my son keep the right perspective in a situation that could bring a great deal of negativity.

The second secret for acquiring the right perspective is gratitude. It is our job to train our kids in the practice of gratitude. Gratitude starts with the parents. This can be especially challenging when we are frustrated with life. We can spend so many of our days striving for a better lifestyle and a more comfortable living situation. In the process, we can become frustrated and shallow in our thinking about our current situation. Even though you may not be where you want to be, you still have so much to be thankful for.

Gratitude can keep you from the inevitable frustration and irritation that accompanies the road to success. You can maintain your focus and instill the right perspective into your kids by maintaining gratitude.

Tony Robbins says, "Where focus goes, energy flows." When your focus is on what you have and not on what you wish you had, it will completely shift your energy. Gratitude will flow easier from you into your environment, to include your children.

There are also other strategies that will help your kids build and maintain a positive attitude. Caleb already addressed this in the book, but I wanted to reiterate it to you. Foods really do affect moods. This is something I frequently told Caleb. Now, he teaches it to kids all over the world.

Healthy and clean eating is essential for a positive attitude. I do not feed Caleb overly processed and sugary food. We drink water with lemons every morning. I also make fresh fruit and vegetable juices each day to increase energy and promote optimal health. During the day, Caleb snacks on raw fruits and vegetables, and he eats at least one salad.

In addition to this, we also do some form of physical activity each day. I make it as fun as possible by incorporating healthy competition. We play baseball, go on runs, rollerblade, play tennis, or do yoga together.

Parents, when you make healthy eating and daily exercise a priority for your family, you will find an overall increase in positive attitudes. You will also become a more emotionally and mentally healthy family as well.

Having a positive attitude must also be paired with self-love. It is so important that your kids love themselves. You should encourage them to take care of their bodies and clean their rooms. Our external and internal conditions play a major role in our attitude and energy.

I stress the importance of self-love to Caleb by requiring that he iron his clothes each morning, make his bed, and take care of his body. In fact, I scheduled a massage for him today because I want him to understand that no matter how hard you work, it should not supersede self-care and self-love.

One of the biggest enemies of self-love is unforgiveness. It can be difficult to love yourself when you are focused on disliking other people. Forgiveness is like a physical detox to the body. Encourage your kids to let go of any anger or unforgiveness they may have towards other people.

Even if they are justified in their anger, that energy will slowly destroy their positive attitude.

Healthy emotions directly affect positivity. That's why it is important to have a great deal of laughing, love, smiling, and affection. Make a lot of memories and have fun even if the budget is tight. Find ways to encourage laughter and happiness in your kids so they can experience the power of a positive attitude.

I'm going to share with you the 5 ways to teach your kids to be positive.

1. Lead by example

I want to ask you a few questions. Are you a positive parent? Do you laugh and enjoy life? Do you release positive energy to your kids? I'll take it a step further. If someone was to ask your kid if they have a positive parent, would they say, yes?

When you lead by example with some of the strategies that I've already shared with you such as having gratitude, being healthy, practicing self-love, and forgiveness, your kids will follow. Remember, you set the tone in your home, so if you are emitting positive energy, your kids will mimic that energy. Our kids are not going to become what we tell them, they are going to become what we show them.

2. Don't allow negative words

If you have more than one kid, I'm sure you've experienced some disagreements and fights between siblings. The words that siblings exchange with one another can be negative at times. I understand that this is a reality. However, when you allow negative words to be spoken, it can be difficult to be a positive family. There should be a rule in your home that bans negativity. In fact, you should put up a sign by the front door that says, "No negativity allowed."

Be strict on your kids about negative talk. It may seem harmless at the time, but it has long term affects that will impact the energy in your home and in your kids. Put consequences in place to communicate the importance of the words that are spoken in the home and towards each other. Only positive speaking and thinking should be acceptable.

3. Only allow positive people around your family

Throughout the years, I've had friends and family members that were negative. I loved them dearly, but I wouldn't allow Caleb to spend a considerable amount of time with them. I'm glad that I moved across the country so that I could create distance between myself and many negative family members.

I love my family, but there were too many of them that maintained a negative energy. I knew that if I allowed my son to constantly be around that energy, it would begin to affect him.

The people that I trust with my son are ones that are kind, complimentary, positive, and forgiving. The people that do not possess these qualities do not have personal access to my son. I would rather risk offense then allow negative energy to become infused into my child.

You are the parent, and you have a responsibility to set the boundary for the type of access you allow others to have with your kids. Your kids come first. If that means that you need to separate your kids from certain family members and friends in order to protect their mindset, then you must do it.

4. Evaluate each other's positivity

I can't stress enough the importance of family meetings. This creates an opportunity for your family to discuss any issues, problems, or triumphs that may be occurring. Imagine if a football team only met once before a big game. Do you think their chances of winning would be high or low?

The reality is that a team can't win unless there is unity, and unity is built through connection and relationships. All great teams meet daily. Caleb's books are a great tool to use so that you can discuss what you are learning as a family.

During the family meetings, you can evaluate one another based on what you are learning. Since this book's focus is on positivity, you can rate each other using that quality. Once again, you can lead by example by asking your kids to rate you. I ask Caleb for his feedback on a regular basis because I want him to see the importance of self-evaluation. I ask,

"On a scale of 1-10, how positive do you think I am, today?"

After Caleb gives me a rating, I ask for further details so that I can make improvements. I then do the same to him. It's not easy, but it is necessary if you want to continuously lead by example. There is nothing more valuable than honest, raw feedback from people that see you every day.

5. Be encouraging and enthusiastic

I believe that we should be our kids' biggest fans. We need to celebrate their strengths and encourage them to conquer their weaknesses. Rather than doing this in a negative, disempowering way, we must become masters of encouragement.

Our kids should feel an energy of enthusiasm coming from us. They must see from our eyes and feel from our souls the belief we have in their ability to become great. I encourage you to continue to verbally express your encouragement, appreciation, and applause for the positive things that your kids do.

One strategy that I used to do with Caleb to enhance his positive attitude was to keep a list of the things he did right throughout the day. At the end of the day, I would share the list with him and tell him how proud of him I was. He would smile and love those moments.

I will leave you with this. Using affirmations and powerful positive quotes in their room will surround your kids with words that will uplift and inspire them daily.

Implementing these strategies and tools will assist in the positive transformation of your kids. It will also help reinforce the information they are receiving from the book. I've personally applied all the information in this chapter. As I stated earlier, Caleb had to deal with the pain of divorce. It was difficult at first, and he went through a period of moodiness and anger. However, when I began to implement these tools and strategies, Caleb's attitude drastically changed.

We continue to use these strategies and have found great success in our relationship and attitudes. I want to implore you to continue to read Caleb's books with your kids, watch his videos, and spend time discussing the information. The investment you make into your kids is the greatest investment you will ever make. I love and believe in you guys. Keep learning, growing, and teaching your kids to be the most positive kids on the planet.

Made in the USA
Middletown, DE
22 May 2020

95811652R00055